No lexile

ILLUSTRATED BY
Martin Chatterton

W9-DBJ-967

DEADLY GAME

TONY BRADMAN

EGMONT

TONY BRADMAN - WORDS

I WAS BORN IN LONDON IN 1954, and was terrified at an early age by a lizard that fell out of a tree that I mistook for a deadly snake; my grandmother, who took snuff and threatened me with a cane when I was naughty; and possible gory death when I ran through the window of a launderette, shattering the glass into tiny pieces with my head. These days I try to avoid things like that, and get most of my frights from watching scary movies and reading scary books. Or writing them.

I still live in London, a dark and ancient city, full of odd corners where nasty things have happened, and where I sometimes worry about bumping into my grandmother's ghost. It hasn't happened yet, but if it does, I might just turn the experience into another 'Tale of Terror'. I hope reading this one scares you as much as writing it terrified me . . .

MARTIN CHATTERTON - PICTURES

IT WAS ALL GOING SO WELL UNTIL Bradman came along . . . An idyllic upbringing in Liverpool. College. Marriage to a devoted wife. Two lovely children. A faithful dog. Twenty years spent quietly illustrating, designing and writing all over the world. I had a good life. A secure, unremarkable, safe existence. And then . . . then . . . Bradman made me work on 'Tales of Terror' and everything changed.

I haven't slept in weeks. I daren't - the nightmares will come back. The voices keep asking me to come out but I won't; not yet. They can't make me. I'm safe in here. Safe with the lights on and the door locked and bolted . . .

Let me give you a word of advice. Come closer. I don't want them to hear. Right up to the crack in the door. I'll whisper it. 'Don't read this book!'

First published 2004
by Egmont Books Limited
239 Kensington High Street, London W8 6SA

Text copyright © 2004 Tony Bradman
Illustrations copyright © 2004 Martin Chatterton

The moral rights of the author and illustrator have been asserted

ISBN 1 4052 1127 X

3 5 7 9 10 8 6 4 2

A CIP catalogue record for this title is available
from the British Library

Printed and bound in Great Britain by the CPI Group

This paperback is sold subject to the condition that it shall not,
by way of trade or otherwise, be lent, resold, hired out, or
otherwise circulated without the publisher's prior consent
in any form of binding or cover other than that in which it
is published and without a similar condition including this
condition being imposed on the subsequent purchaser.

CONTENTS

ONE: VOICES CALLING

Jake is sitting on an old wooden bench in the small back garden of the holiday cottage, reading one of his comics for the umpteenth time, keeping his head down to shield his eyes from the bright morning sunshine. Keeping his head down in another way too. With a bit of luck Mum and Dad and Hannah might leave him alone, and that would suit him just fine.

But soon he can hear noises in the cottage, doors being opened and closed, footsteps, his parents' voices calling, calling. The words are muffled, yet Jake can make them out – 'Jake! Jake, where are you?' He doesn't answer. The bench is hard to see from the bedrooms and the kitchen window. Even so, Jake hunches his shoulders, concentrates more intently on his comic.

Then the back door opens and Dad appears. 'So that's where you've been hiding,' Dad says. 'Come on, we're going out.'

'I don't want to go out,' Jake mutters.

'I'm happy where I am.'

'No choice I'm afraid, pal. We're all in this together. It'll be fun, you'll see.'

Jake raises an eyebrow, gives his father a you-must-be-joking look. But he knows there's not much point in arguing, and closes his comic with a deep sigh. 'That's my boy!' says Dad, smiling at him, and they go inside.

Mum and Hannah are in the hall, Hannah sucking her thumb while Mum fusses over her, making sure she has plenty of suncream on any exposed skin, insisting she wears her hat.

Jake thinks how alike they are, both slim redheads with freckly skin and green eyes. Dad is tall, fair-haired and blue-eyed, and everyone says Jake looks like him, although Jake doesn't agree.

Jake isn't tall for a twelve year old, and his hair is muddy brown, his eyes greeny-grey. He's wearing a red T-shirt and blue jeans, Hannah a yellow dress and white shoes, and their parents are in casual holiday clothes and trainers. Jake notices that Mum doesn't mention suncream or a hat to him.

Hannah takes her thumb from her mouth, smiles at Jake uncertainly.

'We're going to see the stones, Jake,' she says. 'The magic stones.'

Jake ignores her. 'What's happening then?' he says, glancing from Dad to Mum. Hannah's smile fades, and she slips her thumb in her mouth again.

'I wish you wouldn't do that, Jake,'

Mum says, frowning at him.

'Do what?' he says, although he knows perfectly well what she means.

'Treat your sister as if she doesn't exist. I've told you ...'

'We're off to visit the local ancient monument,' Dad says hurriedly, 'which is even older than me, amazingly enough. Right, everybody ready?'

Jake shrugs. Mum shakes her head, and they all go out to the people carrier, Dad taking the driver's seat, Mum next to him, Hannah and Jake in the rear. They drive through the village and turn on to the main road that brought them from the city a few days ago. Jake still has his comic, and he buries his nose in it, trying not to listen as Dad chatters about where they're headed, a stone circle like Stonehenge. Mum doesn't speak, and Jake can tell she's still cross. But then she's always cross with him at the moment.

He looks out of his window at the fields whizzing past, a line of low hills beyond them, a huge, fluffy white cloud hanging motionless in an otherwise clear blue sky. He's glad Dad cut Mum off before she could build up a head of steam. Not that she needs to give him the lecture any

more. Jake knows it by heart – *be nice to Hannah, there's no reason to be horrible to her, she's had enough problems without you adding to them, blah blah blah*. Mind you, Dad could give the same lecture too. He gets just as cross, although lately he's been playing Mr Nice Guy, the family peacemaker.

'You two OK in the back?' says Dad, glancing at them in the rear-view mirror. 'We'll be there soon. It's only a couple of miles from the village.'

'There are *three* of us in the back,' says Hannah in the mock-sulky tone Jake hates. 'And Mr James wants to know where we're having lunch.'

Oh no, not Mr James, thinks Jake. He's been hoping there might be some escape from Hannah's imaginary friend on holiday. At home it's really been getting out of hand, Hannah insisting Mum and Dad set a place for Mr James at every meal, even leave room for him on the sofa when they're watching TV. And to Jake's disgust Mum and Dad have been going along with it.

'You can tell Mr James we've brought a picnic,' says Mum, smiling at her. 'We'll eat it at the stone circle, after we've had a look at everything.'

'Did you hear that, Mr James?' says Hannah, speaking to the empty space between her and her brother. 'A picnic! We can play games as well. I –'

'Isn't she a bit old to have an imaginary friend?' Jake mutters, interrupting her. 'I mean, she's nearly eight. If you ask me it's all a bit creepy.'

'Nobody *was* asking you, Jake,' says Mum, scowling at him, 'and if you've got nothing nice to say about your sister, don't say anything.'

She turns to face forward, and Jake sticks his tongue out at her. Dad spots him in the rear-view mirror and frowns, but Jake doesn't care. He glances at Hannah. Her thumb is planted firmly in her mouth. She's staring at him, and Jake can see in

her eyes that she's not very happy either. Good, he thinks.

A few moments later they pass a sign that tells them they've arrived. They leave the main road and go down a track between hawthorn hedges, finally emerging in a car park which looks pretty full. But Dad finds a space, and they stop.

Jake sees that on the far side of the car park there's a picnic area with a few tables and benches, and beyond them, a dense, shadow-filled grove of trees. On the near side is a small steel and glass building with another sign, one that says *VISITOR CENTRE*. And directly in front of them is a grassy hill, the last and lowest of those Jake had seen from the car. On it stand the ancient stones, dark and massive in the morning sun.

HUMAN SACRIFICES

They get out the car, but to Jake's surprise they don't head straight up the hill. Then he sees that the stones are fenced off, and realises that to reach them you have to pass through the Visitor Centre, which seems very busy. They go in and queue at the ticket desk, where they're served at last by an elderly lady who chats with Mum and Dad and coos soppily over Hannah.

Jake doesn't want to hear any of it, and wanders off on his own.

The building is deceptive, its interior larger than it seems from outside. There are no inner walls. The exhibits and displays are in glass cases or on moveable partitions, and red arrows painted on the floor show you which way to go. At the rear is a cluster of computer terminals, and beyond them a row of tall windows, a glass door in the centre of it leading to the stone circle. Jake follows the arrows, his trainers squeaking faintly on the polished floor, the voices of the people around him muted in the

13

cavernous space.

After a while he reaches the computers. He's not that interested, but he touches an icon on a screen. A picture appears, an artist's impression of a ceremony – a child stretched out on a great stone at the centre of the circle, a man in a dark cloak standing there with his arms raised, a crowd surrounding them. Jake leans forward to examine the man more closely. Is that a knife in one of his hands? The displays had explained that the circle was probably some kind of temple, a place where people had gathered to watch priests performing rituals. They must have gone in for human sacrifices too ...

'Jake! Come on, Jake, we're waiting for you!'

Jake looks round. Mum is standing in the open doorway, silhouetted by the sunlight beyond, her face in shadow. Jake slowly walks over to her. Dad and Hannah are outside, and already some distance along the path that leads from the Visitor

15

Centre to the stone circle. They pause and look back.

'You two carry on ahead,' Mum calls out. 'We'll catch you up!'

Dad waves, then turns and puts an arm around Hannah's shoulders, leaning over her protectively. They resume their climb, and Mum sets off along the path as well. Jake trails after her, a step or two behind, squinting in the sunlight, convinced he's about to get the same old lecture. But he's wrong.

'Listen, Jake,' Mum says. 'If I could change the past, I would. I know things were difficult because of Hannah's illness, and I'm sorry if you felt left out sometimes.' Jake glances at her, doesn't speak. 'I also know lots of brothers and sisters don't get on. But the way you've been acting recently, well …' Mum stops, Jake almost bumping into her. 'Can't you be a bit nicer?' she says, squeezing his shoulder. 'To us, and to Hannah. Life's too short for all this …' She pauses, but he stays silent. 'Think about it, OK?' she says quietly. Then she smiles at him, turns round, walks on up the path.

Jake watches her go, anger flooding through him. It's so easy for her to say those things. A few words, a smile, and suddenly he's supposed to start behaving like the perfect son and brother, is he? Well, maybe he would – if they acted like proper parents to him. He needs some kind of proof that Hannah's not their favourite, that *he* matters to them as much as she does. But they never pay him any attention – except when he's horrible to her.

Which is why he does it, of course, although sometimes he feels a little guilty about his behaviour, a little worried about the kind of person he's becoming. But he's not going to give in to them. Not in a million years. Why should he? *He* didn't bring Hannah into the world. Mum and Dad did ...

He sets off again, trudging up the path in the warm sunshine, his anger hot inside him. The sky is still a brilliant blue; that big, fluffy white cloud moving now, its shadow crossing the side of the hill and sliding up towards the crest, like a great beast swimming through the sea, Jake thinks. He and the shadow reach the entrance to the circle together, and darkness briefly passes over him, a breath of wind ruffling his hair and tugging at his T-shirt.

The entrance is a giant's doorway – two enormous, dark-grey upright stones, at least five metres tall and a couple wide, a third of equal size laid across their tops. Jake stops and looks in. The rest of the circle is made up of similar stones arranged in the same way, although some have fallen and left large gaps. Lots of people are wandering around, little children running and laughing. Jake sees that there's also an inner ring of smaller stones, and glimpses three familiar figures moving within it. His parents and Hannah.

He walks on through the entrance and instantly feels a change in the air, the skin on his face and bare arms tingling, a strange, rather unpleasant sensation. Jake tries to ignore it, thinking it must be to do with the heat, the sun now being directly overhead. But he can't, especially as the feeling grows more powerful with every step he takes deeper into the circle.

He comes to the inner ring, goes inside. And there at the very centre is the stone he saw on the computer. It's almost circular, a metre high and two metres across, and its rough, slightly concave surface is so dark it seems to suck in the sunlight. The tingle in Jake's skin becomes a shudder, and he finds himself thinking there's something about this place he doesn't like.

Dad is kneeling in front of the stone. Mum has her arm round Hannah's shoulders.

'The Heart Stone,' Dad reads from a plaque set in the ground. 'Probably the original altar ... There's a legend that if you touch it when you make a wish, your wish will come true. Oh, there you are, Jake.'

Mum and Hannah look round at Jake, then briefly at each other.

'Just in time!' says Mum. 'Your sister wants me to play hide and seek with her, but I can't run around in this heat. How about you, Jake?'

'Yes, Jake,' says Hannah. 'Will you play with me? Please?'

There is a moment of silence and stillness. Jake looks at his sister, at his parents hanging on his answer. He feels the immensity of the sky above, the brooding presence of the stones around them. A voice deep inside him tries to make itself heard. But his anger is too dark, too bitter, too strong.

'No thanks,' he says. 'I don't play stupid baby games.'

Mum and Dad both scowl and Hannah's face crumbles.

'You're *so* horrible, Jake!' she sobs, and turns away from him. She reaches out to touch the Heart Stone, mumbles something Jake can't hear.

Suddenly, white light explodes in his head and he is falling, falling …

SOUNDLESS SCREAM

After a time Jake realises his eyes are closed and he opens them.

He stares up at pale, ragged clouds streaming across a dark, starless sky, occasional lightning flashes giving them a brief inner glow. Dull, distant rumbles seem to be making the ground tremble beneath him. The ground ... he's lying on the ground. He can feel a pebble pressing painfully into a shoulder blade, grass tickling the soft skin on the inside of a forearm.

He gets to his feet and looks around. There's light coming from somewhere, but it's poor, and shapes are blurred, colours reduced to shades of grey. Jake can see he's alone in the inner ring of the stone circle though. In exactly the same spot he remembers being, in fact, before ...

Before what? Did he pass out? It hadn't felt like that. He casts his mind back, trying to remember the sequence of events. Hannah said something, and he felt as if he were falling, as if a hole had opened beneath him and he'd tumbled into it. Jake looks down at himself. He seems OK. No bones broken, no cuts or bruises. And there are no holes nearby, nothing to explain what happened, where his parents and Hannah might have gone.

Another, brighter flash lights the clouds and there's a deeper rumble, one that vibrates in his bones. A cold gust of wind buffets him and Jake begins to feel afraid. Perhaps a war has started, he thinks. Perhaps the white light was a nuclear explosion; perhaps the falling sensation was caused by a blast; perhaps the flashes and rumbles are more bombs going off; perhaps the clouds are the smoke of burning cities. Perhaps his parents and Hannah and everyone else in the world are dead and he's the last person left alive ...

Jake takes a deep breath, lets it out, forces himself to calm down. There must be a simpler explanation. Then another thought pops into his mind and he feels angry again. Whatever happened, Mum and Dad have obviously run away with their precious Hannah – abandoning *him* to his fate. But that's OK, Jake decides. He can take care of himself. And he'll start by getting out of this creepy place and finding someone who can tell him what's going on.

He strides down the path, away from the Heart Stone and out of the inner ring. There's nobody in the circle, so he goes out the way he came in. He breaks into a jog, heads for the Visitor Centre. The rear door is open, and he steps inside. It's as deserted as the circle, no lights on, the cavernous interior thick with shadows. Jake suddenly feels a surge of fear again, and he pauses for an instant just inside the door, scalp crawling, heart pounding. Then he frowns, tells himself not to be so stupid, makes for the ticket desk.

An enormous flash in the sky outside momentarily floods the entire building with light. The darkness quickly returns, but the brief illumination has allowed Jake to glimpse something that stops him in his tracks.

The picture in the nearest display looks like ... but it can't be!

There are more flashes, and Jake soon sees that it's exactly what he thought – a photograph of his family; Mum and Dad and Hannah and him. A posed shot which seems to have been taken at their cottage that very morning, before they'd set out for the stone circle. But he doesn't remember posing for a picture. Who could have taken it, anyway? More importantly, what is it doing here? Suddenly Jake feels the skin on the back of his neck prickling, and he has an irresistible urge to look over his shoulder …

The computers are glowing, each terminal showing the same picture as the display, his family repeated over and over again on every screen.

Jake's heart is hammering now. He struggles to keep a grip, to stay calm. He turns round, walks on. He notices the red arrows on the floor are glowing too, and that they're pointing in the opposite direction to the way they were earlier. He tries not to think about it, or look at the displays he passes. But each flash outside reveals more pictures of his family, different ones.

Mum and Dad with Jake aged about five, all of them smiling, Mum pregnant; baby Hannah in an incubator, Mum and Dad looking worried; Hannah in hospital for yet another operation to sort out the problem with her kidney; Jake with Nan

and Grandad, staying at their house; Mum
and Dad with Hannah at home, Jake in
the background looking uncertain;
Hannah, a toddler, Jake playing with her;
Hannah in hospital again; Hannah at
home, Mum fussing over her, Jake
scowling; Jake pushing an older Hannah
away, Dad shouting, Jake shouting at him,
Jake being told off by Mum,

Jake sulking, Jake being horrible to Hannah again, and again, and again ...

He stands in front of the last display, scared and horrified and amazed in equal measure. Suddenly the back of his neck prickles once more. He slowly looks round and another flash of lightning reveals the elderly lady in her place behind the ticket desk. But now her face is distorted, her eyes slits of hate, her mouth impossibly wide in a soundless scream, her hair streaming behind her. She moves her hand up in slow motion and points ... at him.

Jake backs away from her, terrified and whimpering. Then he flees, the elderly lady's finger moving to keep pace with him as he runs past her. He slams into the front door, pushes it open, shoots out

into the car park.

That's empty too, every single car that was parked there gone, except for one – their people carrier. It's still in the same spot, looking small and forlorn in the middle of all that open space. Jake pauses, confused, desperately looking round for his family, for anyone. Then he catches sight of a figure walking towards the people carrier – it's Dad! Jake is filled with relief, even though he's angry with his parents, and he runs across the tarmac. He comes up to Dad, slows down, walks along beside him.

'Dad, what's going on?' he gabbles breathlessly. 'Why did you and Mum leave me in the circle? I thought you were ... and something really weird happened in the Visitor Centre, there are these pictures of us, and that lady, she's, she's ...' Jake pauses, his anger flaring. He realises that Dad is taking absolutely no notice, hasn't even looked at him, not once. 'What is this, the silent treatment?' Jake snaps. 'Hello? Dad?' he says, raising his voice.

But Dad still says nothing, still doesn't look at him. He studies Dad's face. Dad is smiling, and now Jake feels more confused, more frightened than ever. It's as if Dad can't see or hear him, as if he's become invisible ... Just then they reach the people carrier and Dad opens the boot. He lifts out the picnic box, closes the boot again, bleeps it locked. He turns and starts walking back in the same direction, goes past Jake. Jake follows him.

'Dad?' Jake says, almost pleading. He stops after a few steps, watches Dad heading towards the picnic area, hears him whistling a jaunty tune.

Jake glances beyond him – and what he sees makes his blood freeze.

DEAD EYES

Three people are sitting at one of the picnic tables, waiting for Dad – Mum, Hannah, and a boy of his own age Jake has never seen before, although he seems familiar. He's staring at Jake across the car park, his face hard, unsmiling. Then the boy turns to Mum, laughs at something she's saying, says something in reply that makes her laugh, although Hannah doesn't.

Jake watches Dad take the picnic box over to them. The boy helps Mum and Dad unpack it and passes a carton of juice to Hannah, just as if he were one of the family. Jake has the strangest feeling as he looks on. Anyone who didn't know them would probably think the boy was Mum and Dad's son, and Hannah's brother. But he's not, Jake tells himself, his anger flooding back, swamping the uneasiness he'd felt at Dad's behaviour. Jake decides this must be a practical joke, some elaborate scheme devised by his parents to make him see the error of his ways. Yes, that's it – those pictures in the Visitor Centre, the elderly lady, it's all a performance for his benefit ...

Well, it's not very funny, Jake thinks. In fact it's cruel, practically child abuse, and he marches across the empty car park to give his parents a piece of his mind. He stops near the picnic table, stands there seething with anger, waits for Mum and Dad to look at him, to acknowledge his presence. But they don't. They carry on with what they're doing as if he wasn't there.

'Hello? Jake calling parents,' he says. There's no reaction. Mum and Dad continue to pass things to Hannah, who's not looking at Jake, and to the boy. He glances at Jake once or twice, but mostly keeps his attention on Mum and Dad.

'Hey!' says Jake, more loudly, standing in his parents' sight line. 'Very funny, Mum and Dad. I know you can see me ...'

He waves both hands at them. Nothing. Mum and Dad and the boy chat and laugh in the way happy families do when they're having a picnic. It's too much for Jake. Doubt fills his mind, and suddenly he feels that he's trapped in a nightmare. His anger and fear boil up inside him, and he opens his mouth to yell and scream ...

'I wouldn't do that if I were you,' says the boy, his voice quiet but firm.

Jake whips round, glares across the table. The boy meets his gaze calmly. Jake sees now that he's much the same size as him, and wearing the same kind of T-shirt as he is, although the boy's is blue. 'What business is it of yours what I do?' Jake snaps. 'And who the hell are you, anyway?'

'Why, Jake,' says the boy, a mocking smile playing round his lips. 'I'm surprised you haven't guessed. You must be even more of a moron than I took you for. Oh well … shall I tell him, Hannah, or will you?' Jake catches Hannah staring at him, a strange, almost fearful expression on her face. But all Jake can think is that she can see him … 'OK, I'll do it then,' says the boy, his voice breaking into Jake's thoughts. 'I'm afraid there's no easy way to put this, Jake, so I'll just have to be brutal. I'm your replacement.'

'My … replacement?' says Jake. 'What are you talking about?'

'I'm in and you're out,' says the boy, shrugging. 'I'm Mum and Dad's son now, and Hannah's big brother, and you're not any more. That's about as simple as I can make it. I've even got your comic,' he says, pulling it from his back pocket and tossing it on the table. 'Although I must say I'm not very impressed by your taste in reading matter ... OK, I think that covers everything. I suggest you disappear and let us get on with our picnic ...'

'Whoa there!' says Jake. 'You're having me on, aren't you?'

The boy sighs, shakes his head. 'No, Jake, I'm not,' he says. 'But I can see you won't get this until I lay the whole thing out for you. Remember when Hannah asked you to play hide and seek with her in the circle and you said no? That upset her, so she wished that her imaginary friend could be her brother instead of you. And because she touched the Heart Stone at the same time, her wish came true. I'm right, aren't I, Hannah?' Hannah looks up from her paper plate, glances at him and at Jake. She nods, looks down at her plate again. 'So zap, pow, alakazam ...' says the boy, 'here I am.'

'That's crazy,' Jake murmurs, but there's an unsettling quality about the boy's confidence. Jake studies him closely for the first time and realises he seems familiar because there's a strong family

resemblance between them. In fact, they could easily be taken for brothers. Except for one thing. The boy's eyes aren't blue like Dad's, or green like Mum's and Hannah's, or even greeny-grey like Jake's. His eyes are cold, flat, colourless. Dead eyes, Jake thinks. 'So you're telling me you're Mr James, and that you've magically been made into a real person?' Jake says, trying to keep his voice steady, and failing. 'It's like something from a fairy tale. It can't happen.'

'Oh, but it has, Jake,' says the boy. 'And it's just plain James, actually. Hannah and I decided to drop the Mr, didn't we, sis?' Hannah says nothing, slips her thumb into her mouth. 'I know it's hard to believe, Jake. But you should bear in mind there's a lot of power in an ancient site like this. Come on, accept it. What other explanation could there be, anyway? Take a peep at yourself if you want more proof. There's more light here to see by.'

Jake does as he's told, and his heart seems to stop when he realises that his T-shirt, his jeans, his trainers are still grey, even in better light – material, stitching, buttons, leather, laces, everything. Exactly the same shade of grey.

'Oh dear, Jake,' says the boy. 'You look as though you've seen a ghost.'

LOST SOULS

Jake tries to speak, but no words come out. He looks up, allows the utter weirdness of his surroundings to sink in. The eerie light that fills the picnic area though the sky is dark, his parents behaving as if nothing strange were happening, the boy – or rather *James* – watching him with his dead eyes.

This isn't a practical joke or an elaborate hoax, Jake thinks. It's not a hallucination, either, not a dream or a nightmare. It's terrifyingly real.

'Ah, I do believe we're reading from the same page at last,' says James. 'Is there anything else you'd like to know? Any details I can fill in for you?'

'What's happened to me?' says Jake. 'Why are my clothes all grey?'

'That's because you're in a different world,' says James. 'Or perhaps I should call it a different dimension. Whatever, it's where imaginary friends lead their poor, thin, sad existences. A place with no life, and no colour.'

'But you're not all grey ...' says Jake. He glances at his sister. She's following the conversation, her eyes flicking between the two boys. 'Wait a minute – how come you and Hannah can see me but Mum and Dad can't? And why aren't they taking any notice of you and what you're saying?'

'You really are a bit slow on the uptake, Jake, aren't you?' says James. 'Look, *you're* the imaginary friend now, OK?' He talks slowly, as if he's speaking to a toddler, Jake realises. And not a very bright toddler at that, either. 'So Hannah can see you, of course, and I can too. But Mum and Dad can't because they're grown-ups, and everybody knows that grown-ups don't have imaginary friends. And they don't take much notice of us kids when they think we're playing, especially if we're not bothering them.'

James leans back and folds his arms, a smug expression on his face, challenging Jake to disagree, to prove him wrong. But Jake isn't going to.

'OK, I believe you,' Jake murmurs. 'It's

seriously weird, but not much more than the idea of a wish actually coming true. 'So how long will it be before things return to normal? Before I get out of this ... dimension?'

'I wouldn't hold your breath,' says James. 'I think you should probably plan on a fairly lengthy stay. Actually, the word *forever* comes to mind.'

A chill runs down Jake's spine, and he swallows, his throat tight.

'Forever?' he asks, his voice sounding very small. There's a bright flash in the sky above, a deep, distant rumble. 'But what am I supposed to do?'

'Do?' says James. He gets up, walks round the table and past Hannah, his face suddenly hard and unsmiling again. He stands in front of Jake. 'As an imaginary friend you don't *do* anything. Oh, you hang around, you listen and sympathise and, finally, when the time comes, when Hannah grows out of the imaginary friend stage and doesn't need you any more ...' He pauses, raises a hand, flutters his fingers and makes a slow, falling gesture. He smiles, his dead eyes fixed on Jake's. 'Well then, you simply fade away.'

'I don't understand,' says Jake. 'Do you mean I'm going ... to die?'

'Oh no,' says James. 'It's far worse than that. Once you lose your reason for being, you become one of the lost souls, forever trapped in nothingness. There are a few over there in the trees, Jake. Take a look at your future.'

Jake turns and peers at the glade behind the picnic area. At first all he can make out is dense shadow, dark trunks, branches with stiff black leaves that rattle in a brief gust of wind. Then he begins to make out dim, grey shapes flitting and swooping between the trees. He hears them hissing, whispering, sees them gathering at the edge of the glade, watching him, waiting …

Jake catches his breath, whimpers again, steps backwards.

'I'm not going to end up in there,' he mutters. 'Not like *them*.'

'You don't have a lot of choice,' says James. 'You're ...'

'Just be quiet, will you?' says Jake, his anger flaring inside him once more. He glimpses Hannah staring at him from behind James, and pushes past him, walking round the table to stand over her. 'So I've got you to thank for this, have I?' he says. Hannah sucks her thumb harder, lowers her head and looks up at him, her eyes wide. 'For being trapped here forever, for fading away? Well, cheers, Hannah, that's terrific. I suppose I should have known you'd manage to get rid of me eventually. Some sister *you* are.'

Hannah winces at every word, then lowers her eyes and looks away.

'Temper, temper,' says James. 'You really should try to develop more self-control, Jake. It might help you to avoid saying things you'll regret.'

'*Now* what are you talking about?' Jake glares at him.

'Perhaps I should have told you earlier,' says James. 'Actually, there *is* a way out of all this. But it's the only way, and I have a feeling you might just have blown it.' He pauses, a smile on his face. Jake waits, his mouth dry, his heart pounding, a pulse beating like a drum in his head. 'It's rather simple,' says James. 'Hannah made the wish. So Hannah can unmake it too.'

James turns to her. 'Although you probably don't want to now, do you, sis?'

Hannah looks up at Jake again – and suddenly he feels sick …

TURNING POINT

Jake stands there, his stomach churning, his mind in a whirl. He feels he should say something, take back what he said to Hannah, but he doesn't know where to start. He looks at her, opens his mouth, closes it again.

'I'm impressed, Jake,' says James. 'What a terrific impersonation of a fish! Or maybe you're just lost for words ... I would be, if I were you.'

Jake grits his teeth, clenches his fists. He's had enough of being taunted by this imposter. 'Well, you're not me,' he says, taking a couple of steps towards the other boy. Jake gives him his hardest, meanest playground stare. 'And you're not taking *my* place in *my* family,' he adds. 'Got that?'

'Ooooh,' says James. 'I'm really scared ... er, not. But I tell you what. I'll give you a chance. Hannah can choose which of us she wants as her brother, OK? We'll each put our case, then Hannah can decide between us, and the loser has to accept defeat. You'll go along with that, won't you, Hannah?'

Hannah looks at Jake, then back at James. She nods, slipping her thumb in her mouth immediately afterwards. James turns to Jake and smirks at him.

'So … how about it, Jake?' he says. 'You don't have much to lose.'

Jake's stomach twists, and his mouth fills with the warm, bitter taste of fear. He knows this is the turning point, that his whole life is held in the balance at this moment. He looks at Mum and Dad. They're still sitting at the table, eating and talking quietly to each other, oblivious to what's happening. What did Dad say about their outing today? That it would be fun ... Well, you were wrong, Dad, Jake thinks. He takes a deep breath and turns to face James.

'OK, it's a deal,' he says, with far more confidence than he feels.

'Right, let's give ourselves some room,' says James. He strides away from the picnic area, gesturing to Hannah to follow him, which she does, giving Jake a strange

62

backward glance he can't interpret, her eyes briefly locking on his. Jake follows, stops when James and Hannah do, the three of them forming a rough triangle, Hannah at the apex, James and Jake at either ends of the base. 'Well, here we are, all nicely in position,' says James. 'I suppose we should toss a coin to see who goes first. Have you got a coin, Jake?'

'I ... I don't think so,' says Jake, patting the pockets of his jeans.

'I'll go first then,' says James. He turns to Hannah, squares his shoulders, gathers himself like an actor preparing to give an important speech in a play.

'Hannah,' he says, smiling, drawing out her name, his voice caressing it, 'we haven't known each other long, not properly, anyway. But you know I've always been there for you, and I think you've realised now that I'm a much better prospect as a big brother than Jake … who's a total waste of space.'

'Hey, that's not fair,' Jake yells. 'You're just running me down!'

'All's fair in love and families, Jakey boy,' James snaps. 'And I'm only telling the truth. You *are* a total waste of space. You've been horrible to Hannah since the day she was born, and mean to Mum and Dad. You're eaten up inside with jealousy, you're vicious and vile and selfish …'

DEADLY
GAME

Jake listens as James lists his bad qualities, all the bad things he's done, the relentless voice finding the part of him that feels guilty, oh so guilty. Jake looks up at the clouds streaming across the dark sky, sees the flashes, hears the rumbles, and suddenly his mind isn't in a whirl any more. His anger disappears and he's convinced that everything James says is right. Of course Mum and Dad were worried about Hannah. She'd nearly died, for God's sake! But what had *he* done? Made their lives miserable with his constant demands for attention. So what kind of person behaves like that? The kind of person who doesn't deserve to be part of a good family ...

'OK, OK,' Jake says at last, looking

down, stopping James in mid-rant. 'I've heard enough,' he whispers. 'More than enough. You win ...'

'Really?' says James. 'You mean you don't you want to try and put your case?' Jake shakes his head. 'You're absolutely *sure*?' Jake nods.

James closes his eyes, tips his head back for a second, breathes deeply.

'Yes ...!' he hisses, then smiles and opens his eyes. Jake can see they're not flat and colourless any more. They're shiny, black and glinting with triumph.

'Good call, Jake,' James says after a moment. 'Now why don't you just run along? You said yourself that Hannah's too old for an imaginary friend, so you're not needed any more. I feel a clean break would be best, don't you?

'I'm going,' says Jake. He looks at the trees, sees the grey shapes waiting. He shivers, but his mind is made up. 'Is it OK if I say goodbye though?'

'Be my guest,' says James. 'But don't drag it out.'

Hannah hasn't moved. Jake starts walking towards her, then stops. Her little face is sad and Jake can feel his eyes prickling. 'I'm sorry, Hannah. For everything. I should have been nicer to you. You'll be much happier without me around. Take care of yourself, OK?' Jake isn't sure, but he thinks Hannah's bottom lip is trembling. He quickly turns away, heads for the picnic area, stands in front of Mum and Dad. 'I should have been a

better son to you too,' he whispers, a tear spilling on to his cheek. 'I'm sorry ...'

Mum and Dad are talking quietly, but suddenly they both go very still.

They turn slowly to face him. They're squinting, peering like people trying to see through a mist. 'Jake ... is that you?' Mum says hesitantly, and now Jake is certain they've heard him, that they can see him too. But then the moment passes and they look away as if he's become invisible again.

'Come on, Jakey boy, hurry up,' snarls James. 'Just go, will you?'

Jake glares at him, new questions already forming on his lips, his anger welling up inside him again. But then something else surprising happens.

Hannah speaks.

DEADLY GAME

'I don't want Jake to go,' she says, her small, pure voice carrying clearly across the empty car park. Jake looks at his little sister in her yellow dress, immense darkness above and beyond her, and he realises how tiny and vulnerable she is.

But there's determination in her face too, her eyes fierce with it. 'He can't go,' she says. 'I haven't done the choosing yet.'

'But you don't need to,' says James. 'Jake's already done it for you ...'

'That doesn't matter,' Hannah says firmly. 'You said *I* had to do it.'

'OK then, sweetheart,' James says, briefly giving her a cold smile. 'Let's hear your big decision. I hope you've been thinking about it *very* hard.'

'I have,' says Hannah. 'I choose ... Jake to be my brother.' A huge flash fills the sky, followed by an enormous rumble.

Hannah runs to Jake and looks up into his eyes. 'I'm sorry too, Jake,' she says, the words tumbling from her. 'But you were horrible, and I made the wish and you fell over and Mr James came and I thought he was nice, but he isn't, he's different and he's creepy and more horrible than you ever were, and I don't like him, and then you said you were sorry so I knew you were nice, but I always did ...'

'It's OK, Hannah,' Jake says. 'You've got nothing to be sorry for.' He draws her close, his guilt deepening. He should have realised she'd been terrified by the consequences of her wish ... and suddenly he knows what else he wants to say. 'It's going to be different from now on, Hannah, I promise,' he whispers. '*I'm* going to be different. I'll look after you. All you have to do is unmake your wish, then everything will be all right ...'

'Ah, how sweet,' says a voice. Jake looks

round. James is watching them, his smile even colder than before. 'A touching scene … and a classic happy ending to your story,' he says. 'It's such a pity I'll have to spoil it.'

'You leave us alone,' says Jake, scowling at the other boy. 'We made a deal, remember? Hannah's chosen me, and you have to accept defeat.'

James laughs at him. 'You're crazy if you think I'm going back to being Mr James,' he says. 'Grey isn't my colour, and I'm far too young to fade away. I'm very disappointed in you, Hannah. This could all have been so easy. Now I suppose I'll just have to switch to Plan B, unluckily for you …'

'We're not listening,' says Jake. 'Come

on, Hannah, let's go.'

'Stop right there,' James says, his voice suddenly harsh and menacing. 'You two aren't going anywhere. Plan B involves me killing Hannah, for obvious reasons.' Jake feels Hannah breathe in sharply, her small body trembling, and he grips her shoulder. 'But I'm afraid I'm going to have to kill you first, Jake. Mum and Dad are very attached to you. They were both so moved by your farewell speech I thought for a second they might pull you back into the real world. Which means I can't take the risk of you being left hanging around after I've disposed of Hannah, not even as a lost soul ...'

So they do love me, Jake realises. James has just given him something he's wanted for a long time, real proof that Mum and Dad do care about him. All his anger and resentment fade away and he feels oddly calm. Then Hannah squeezes his hand, looks up at him and he focuses on James once more.

'Take your best shot, pal,' Jake says, pushing Hannah behind him. 'I can handle you, no problem.' He's sure he could beat James in a straight fight. They're the same size, after all. Or at least they were ...

'I don't think so,' says James, and grins at them. He starts to grow, and soon doubles in size, his arms and shoulders rippling with muscle, his hands huge. He looms over them, his face terrifying, evil. Hannah screams, and Jake gasps.

'But let's make this fun, shall we?' says James. 'You said you don't play stupid baby games, Jake. Well, let's play a deadly game of hide and seek. You run off and hide while I count to ten. One, two, three …'

Jake turns and flees, grabbing Hannah's hand and pulling her with him, making for the Visitor Centre. They go in, and Jake shuts the main door and drags a rack of leaflets in front of it. That ought to give them some time …

It's just as before inside the building, the thick darkness driven back every so often by the flashes in the sky. The elderly lady is still at the ticket desk, but now she's holding her face with both hands, her eyes impossibly wide in fear, her mouth still distorted in a soundless howl of horror. Jake runs on with Hannah, past the exhibits and displays, past the glowing computer screens, each one showing a new picture now – Mum and Dad with James, all three of them smiling happily, no Jake and Hannah to be seen.

There's a sound of smashing glass as the main door is kicked in. Jake looks round just as a colossal flash floods the building with light. James is there behind them, his enormous shadow stretching long, groping hands across the floor in their direction. Then the darkness swoops down again.

'Ready or not, here I come!' James calls out, and laughs wildly.

Jake and Hannah are already running up the path to the stones.

EVIL VOICE

They hurry through the entrance to the circle, huge flashes splitting the sky above them, the ground trembling with the rumbles that follow. Jake's eyes are fixed on the inner ring and the dark bulk of the Heart Stone within it, and he speeds up, dragging Hannah along. He can hear her panting, his own breath coming in gasps, a solid, tight fist of pain beneath his breastbone.

He doesn't dare look back. He doesn't want to know how close behind James might be ... Nearly there, Jake thinks, as they reach the inner ring. Just a few metres more and Hannah can unmake her wish and they'll be safe.

Jake skids to a halt in the open space surrounding the Heart Stone, his trainers slipping on the grass, Hannah almost falling. Something doesn't feel right. He pulls Hannah close and looks around, trying to get his breathing under control, stop his heart pounding. It's as if they're being watched, Jake thinks, his skin tingling as it did when he first entered the circle. He can hear whispering too, a soft, evil voice hissing at them from every direction.

'*Jake* ...' the voice says, drawing his name out till it sounds like a dying breath. '*Hannah ... There's no hiding place in there. No hiding place at all ...*'

And then there's that wild laughter again, echoing round the stones.

'I don't like it, Jake,' says Hannah, her fingers digging into his arm.

'It's OK, Hannah,' Jake murmurs, a huge flash of lightning allowing him to scan the gaps between the inner stones. 'I can't see him anywhere ...'

Jake turns, starts to lead Hannah towards the Heart Stone. The next flash reveals it, barely a few metres in front of them. Darkness falls once more, swiftly followed by another flash from above. And now a tall, dark-cloaked figure is standing between them and the Heart Stone, its head lowered. But then the figure slowly looks up … and Jake sees that it's James.

A grinning James, who raises the cloak with both arms wide and laughs.

Jake is rigid with shock, and Hannah buries her face in his T-shirt.

'Boo,' James says quietly. 'Found you ... So it looks like I've won.'

'But ... how did you get here?' says Jake. 'You were behind us.'

'Oh, I'm full of tricks,' says James. 'Anyway, like the outfit? Pretty cool, isn't it? I told you there's plenty of power in this circle. But there are plenty of ghosts too, and I've learned a lot from one, a priest who used to have a special job here a long time ago. He's been helping me to see things a lot differently. You could even say I've incorporated him into my act. Maybe that's why I'm not the quiet, inoffensive little friend I used to be …'

James strides forward and yanks Hannah from Jake's grasp as if she's a rag doll. She screams and struggles, but James soon puts a stop to that. He pulls her tight against him, a powerful arm across the throat silencing her.

'Leave her alone!' Jake yells, his voice almost breaking. 'Or I'll …'

'Relax, Jake,' James says softly. 'I've just had a great idea. I could make you *my* imaginary friend once I've got rid of Hannah, and then it would be just us, two boys together with no sister taking all Mum and Dad's attention. How about it … brother?' Suddenly James is holding a knife in his other hand, its leaf-shaped bronze blade glinting dully in a flash of lightning. James presses the point against Hannah's throat, his eyes on Jake. 'One little nick in Hannah's skin,' James murmurs, 'a few drops of blood and she's gone forever. And that's what you wanted, wasn't it, Jake? Hannah to die ...'

Until then Jake has been trembling all over, but now he feels the shaking subside, his body go still as he stands there beneath James's gaze. Is it true? Had he wanted Hannah to die? He'd certainly hated her at times, but only because of what had happened, all the disruption and worry. And maybe once or twice he'd wished she'd never been born. But wanting her to die …? Jake looks at his little sister, sees the fear in her eyes, but also a look that says she trusts him, and he knows that he loves her and wants her to live.

'No deal, *Mr* James,' says Jake. 'You've got me completely wrong.'

Hannah smiles at him, then opens her mouth, shows her small white teeth. She quickly flicks her eyes down at James's bare arm, then back up at Jake, and he gives her the tiniest of nods, understanding immediately what she's suggesting. But he also raises his hand slightly by his side, the fingers spread out, a warning to her to wait for the right moment, hoping James doesn't see.

Something is happening to distract James though. There's a rustling, a soft whispering like the sound of the wind sighing through a field of wheat.

James is looking at the gaps between the stones, and Jake does as well. Grey shapes drift through and gather in the space around the Heart Stone. Soon James and Jake and Hannah are surrounded by a ghostly host, the phantoms jostling for position, their spectral eyes bright stars

in a wavering mist.

'It seems we have an audience for the grand finale,' says James, smiling. 'Hardly surprising, really. This must be the most exciting thing to happen here for at least a couple of thousand years.' He turns his attention to Jake again. 'I'm disappointed in you too,' he says, taking the knife away from Hannah's throat and pointing it at Jake. 'You and your sister make a good pair. Neither of you can recognise a great opportunity when it's offered ...'

'Now, Hannah!' Jake yells, and Hannah instantly sinks her teeth into James's arm, biting deep with all her might, her eyes bulging with effort.

James looks down at her, utterly astonished, and he howls in pain.

'Why, you little ...' he hisses, and throws her from him. She lands near the Heart Stone, rolls over a couple of times and scrambles to her feet.

'Quick, Hannah!' Jake almost screams at her. 'Unmake the wish ...'

James is examining his arm, but looks up at Jake's words and realises what's happening. He moves forward, his face full of hate and violence, and Jake runs to meet him, seizing his knife arm, kicking out at him with his trainers, trying to give Hannah the time she needs. But James is far too strong, and grabs the front of Jake's T-shirt with his other hand, gathering a fistful of material and lifting him clean off the ground. James holds him in mid-air for a second, then slams him down on the Heart Stone and pins him there.

The impact drives the breath from Jake's body, but he still scrabbles at James's hand with his nails, and wriggles and kicks. It's no use. James bears down on him and Jake feels himself being crushed, his spine being ground into the rock beneath him, his ribs about to crack under the pressure.

Jake looks up at last, into the face of evil. James is grinning again. He tightens his grip on Jake's T-shirt and slowly raises his other arm on high. The leaf-shaped blade gleams in a colossal, sky-splitting flash of lightning.

'Game over, Jakey boy,' James murmurs, his black eyes glinting. He swings the knife down, the ghostly crowd letting out a sigh of pleasure.

Jake turns his head away, sees Hannah reaching towards the Heart Stone, screaming something he can't hear, her fingers a hair's breadth from the rock.

Suddenly, white light explodes in Jake's head, and he is falling, falling ...

Epilogue

After a time, Jake realises his eyes are closed and he opens them. He sees three faces above him, two large and one small, each wearing an expression of concern. Mum, Dad and Hannah, an enormous blue sky behind them.

'He's coming round,' says Mum, and she and Dad help him sit up. 'Are you OK, love?' says Mum. 'You went down like you'd been pole-axed.'

'I'm fine, Mum,' says Jake, and gets to his feet, Mum and Dad holding on to him. Jake checks himself over. Red T-shirt, blue jeans, white trainers. Then he checks the surroundings. The four of them are near the Heart Stone, and the sky is full of warm sunshine, exactly the way it was when they arrived, except that the big, fluffy white cloud has vanished. But James has gone too, and so have the ghosts. Finally Jake checks his sister. He notices a faint red mark on the pale skin of her neck, but otherwise she seems perfectly all right. Their eyes meet and she smiles. 'I just felt a bit ... odd,' Jake says.

'You've probably had too much sun,' says Dad. 'It's very hot.'

'Oh, Jake,' Mum says suddenly, guilt and anguish in her voice. She puts a cool hand on his forehead to feel whether he's got a temperature. 'You should be wearing a hat on a day like this, and suncream, like Hannah. I'm so sorry, love. We don't seem to have been taking proper care of you recently ...'

'Don't worry about it, Mum,' says Jake. 'It wasn't your fault.'

'You're sure you feel OK?' says Mum. 'Not dizzy, or sick, or …'

'No, Mum, honest,' says Jake. 'Really, I've never felt better.'

'That's good,' Mum says. 'I'll keep an eye on you, just the same.' She looks deep into his eyes. Then she smiles and kisses his cheek.

'I think you might be hungry, as well,' says Dad. 'I know I am. In fact, I'm absolutely starving. And we've had our dose of history for today. Those in favour of supper at that pizza place we saw yesterday, follow me.'

So the family leaves the inner ring, Mum with her arm around Jake's shoulders, Dad in front with Hannah, both of them looking back at Jake from time to time, concern still in their eyes. They reach the Visitor Centre, Jake feeling nervous as they enter, afraid of what he might see. But everything is as it should be – families milling around the exhibits, the elderly lady at the ticket desk back to normal. She cheerily bids them goodbye as they go out.

The car park is busy again. Dad unlocks

the people carrier, and they get into their familiar seats. Dad starts the engine, and they drive off, leaving the stones behind. Jake looks at the grove of trees. A gust of wind swishes through the branches and across a picnic table, angrily flicking open the pages of a comic somebody has left there. Jake doesn't ask Dad to stop.

'You two OK in the back?' Dad says, his eyes on Jake and Hannah in the rear-view mirror. Mum turns round as well. 'Or should I say you three?'

'There's only two of us,' Hannah says firmly. Then she peeks at Jake across the small space between them. 'Just me ... and my horrible brother.'

But she grins as she says it. Jake reaches over and tickles her, and she squeals and squirms away from him, and he laughs. Mum and Dad glance at each other, and raise their eyebrows in surprise. Then they laugh too.

Jake is still smiling as they turn on to the main road and head for the pizza place, the tyres thrumming smoothly on the tarmac beneath him.

He's sure the rest of the day is going to be a lot of fun, after all.

ALSO BY
TONY BRADMAN